MARY-KATE & ASHLEY

Starring in

THE CHALLENGE

A novelization by Megan Stine

Story by Michael Swerdlick

Based on the screenplay by Michael Swerdlick
and Elizabeth Kruger

HarperEntertainment
An Imprint of HarperCollins*Publishers*

A PARACHUTE PRESS BOOK

PARACHUTE PRESS

Parachute Publishing, L.L.C.
156 Fifth Avenue
New York, NY 10010

DUALSTAR PUBLICATIONS

Dualstar Publications
c/o Thorne and Company
1801 Century Park East
Los Angeles, CA 90067

HarperEntertainment

An Imprint of HarperCollins*Publishers*
10 East 53rd Street, New York, NY 10022

CHAPTER ONE

"I need a gimmick!" television host Max Trevor cried in his production office in Hollywood. "The ratings are down. We've got to do something soon or the network will cancel our show!"

"Calm down, Max," his assistant, Sasha, said.

"I can't calm down, Sash!" Max screamed. "We need more people to watch *The Challenge* or we're history!"

Marcus Wilson stood in the doorway to Max's office with two videotapes in his hands. The eighteen-year-old intern smiled to himself. The famous Max Trevor was in trouble, and Marcus was going to save his show! "I think I've got something you should see," he said, marching over to the two VCRs in Max's office. He popped a videotape into each one.

He'd been working as a paid intern for a few weeks on *The Challenge*, the reality TV show Max produced and hosted. Most of Marcus's time was spent copying scripts and fetching coffee. But his favorite part of the job was screening audition tapes. They came in from high school students who wanted to be on the show.

Okay, so maybe *The Challenge* was a lot like

other reality-based TV shows set in tropical paradises where a group of people had to eat slime to stay alive. But there was one thing that set it apart: the prize. A full college scholarship for every contestant on the winning team.

"Check this out," Marcus said as he flipped on the VCR and started the first tape.

Max and Sasha stared at the beautiful young blond on the screen. She was wearing a chic black sweater and short leather skirt. "Hi, I'm Lizzie Dalton, from Washington, D.C.," the girl said. "And I'm ready for *The Challenge*!"

Marcus pushed PAUSE to freeze-frame on her face. Then he clicked the remote for the second VCR. It was another audition tape, but the girl on it looked just like Lizzie. Only *this* girl had her blond hair in braids, and she was wearing a funky tie-dyed shirt over a peasant skirt.

"Hi, I'm Shane Dalton, from L.A., and I'm ready for *The Challenge*!" The girl smiled, raised two fingers in the air, and gave the peace sign.

Max shook his head. "She has a split personality," he said. "That's so sad. She can't go to college."

"Wake up, Max," Sasha said. "They're twins! This could be perfect!"

"It's more than perfect," Marcus explained. "The parents are divorced. Shane lives with the mother in Los Angeles, California. Lizzie lives with the father in Washington, D.C. And they're *total* opposites."

Max leaned forward in his seat. "Tell me more."

"Well, Lizzie's into ambition," Marcus went on. "The other one, nutrition. Lizzie wants to hang out with political types at Georgetown U. The other one is a vegetarian who wants to go to Berkeley. If my radar is right, I'm guessing these two sisters hate each other."

Max jumped up. "Marcus, you're a genius!" He clapped him on the back. "And you know what else? If this sisters-who-hate-each-other thing works, I'll give you an extra five thousand bucks as a bonus."

"Seriously?" Marcus's eyes opened wide. He could really use the money for college in the fall.

Max nodded. "Book these girls for the show," he said, "and when we start production, I want you to get all the dirt on them. You're my spy, understand?"

"Yeah," Marcus said, feeling a little funny about that part. It was one thing to set these girls up. It was another to spy on them. But it was all part of the job, right? "Okay, I'm your spy," he agreed.

"What is this place—paradise?" Shane Dalton asked, stepping onto the set of *The Challenge*. She gazed around at the exotic flowering plants that surrounded the resort hotel in Cabo San Lucas, Mexico.

"I could live here the rest of my life!" the girl

next to Shane said as they walked down a stone path toward the beach.

No kidding, Shane thought. The sun was almost setting in the distance, and it cast a beautiful red-orange glow on everything. At the end of the path was a circle of tiki torches surrounding benches made out of logs. In the center Shane saw a big pit of fire.

That's it, she thought, immediately recognizing the set of the Campfire Council from the television show *The Challenge*.

Five other teenagers were already in the circle when Shane and the other girl arrived. Shane glanced at them, wondering which ones would be on her team.

A guy with stylish brown hair and the cutest dimples Shane had ever seen flashed her a grin.

Shane smiled back. *If we're choosing up sides, I pick* him, she thought.

"I'm JJ," the girl walking beside Shane said, tossing her long dark hair over her blue sequined halter top. She was wearing tight jeans and strappy black heels that clicked on the stone walkway. "I'm from Miami Beach."

"Hi," Shane said. "Shane Dalton. Los Angeles."

A guy with sun-bleached surfer hair jumped up and jerked his thumb toward the water. "Check it out! The ocean's right there!" he said. "Man, Jet-Skis! Parasailing! This is the bomb!"

"We're not here for a vacation," a girl with silky brown hair snapped. She was tan, buff, and toned. "We're here to take—"

"*The Challenge!*" Shane and the others all blurted out, laughing. It was the tag line from the show. All the Warriors from *The Challenge* said it at least five times per episode.

Shane gazed out at the water. She could hardly believe she was on the beach in Mexico—or that she was a contestant on a reality TV show. After all, she was all about being in touch with her inner *chi* and holding onto her spiritual calm—not competition.

This was more the kind of thing her twin sister would be into. Not that Shane really cared what her sister was into anymore. The two of them hadn't seen or spoken to each other since their parents got divorced two years ago.

"So what's your talent?" JJ asked.

"My talent?" Shane was surprised. "I didn't know you had to have one. This isn't a beauty contest or anything, is it?"

JJ opened her mouth to answer, but just then they both noticed a huge scruffy man moving around to Shane's left. He was wearing a black *The Challenge* T-shirt and carrying a professional video camera on his shoulder. He had the thing aimed right at her.

"Oh, wow. Are we being taped?" Shane asked.

"I'm Big Joe," the man said. "Just ignore me." He swung the camera toward JJ. "Don't look at the camera unless you're being interviewed."

Weird, Shane thought. It was hard to pretend this guy wasn't right in her face—although she and the others had been told that from the minute they stepped off the bus at the resort hotel they would be videotaped for the show.

JJ flashed the camera a huge smile and then pretended to ignore it. "I'm a singer-dancer-actor," she gushed to Shane. "I'm going to Juilliard next year— if I win."

"Cool," Shane said as they each took a seat on one of the benches for the Campfire Council. A moment later a good-looking man came walking toward them.

"Hello, everyone," the man called.

Shane instantly recognized Max Trevor, the host of *The Challenge*. He was wearing his trademark stretch white T-shirt. His hair looked as if it had so much styling gel in it, you couldn't mess it up with a fire hose.

Max quickly introduced his assistant, Sasha, and his intern, a cute guy named Marcus. Then he said, "Okay, people, I'm glad you're here. We'll start shooting the opening with each of you Warriors in just a moment." Max waved his arms at the big guy with the black T-shirt and video camera.

The man crouched low in front of Max. Ten or

twelve other production crew people scurried around the host. Some of them were doing sound checks. Others were setting up lights.

"You ready?" the big guy asked Max.

"Let's do it," Max said as the lights dimmed

The cameraman crouched even lower, and someone called, "Rolling!"

"Welcome to *The Challenge*," Max said into the camera, "where students from across the country compete for college scholarships in daring tests of survival and knowledge. . . ."

Shane shot a glance at JJ and stifled a laugh. She had seen the show enough times to know that when this opening aired on TV, it would have hokey flute music playing in the background.

Max put on his most dramatic voice and stared into the camera. "Are *you* ready for . . . *The Challenge*?"

I hope so! Shane thought, crossing her fingers for luck.

Then the crew started bustling around, steering the contestants into place for their personal interviews.

A tall, dark-haired guy with a goofy smile went first. He wore a red bandanna on his head, pirate style. "I'm Anthony Rigoletti," he said. "And I want to go to a college with a good culinary program. I'm gonna be a chef, like that Emeril guy. Bam!"

"Excellent!" Max said, clapping.

The surfer kid took his spot next in front of the camera. "Justin Tyler. M.I.T., dude. Astrophysics. Solid!"

While JJ was setting up for her on-camera interview, Shane turned to meet the others. The cutie with the dimples was Adam. He was planning to go to Stanford.

"What's your major going to be?" Shane asked him.

"Journalism," Adam said. "After that I want to play a little and see the world."

"Travel? Me, too," Shane said. "Once school is over."

Adam shot her another grin and their eyes locked.

Her heart skipped a beat. There was something about him. He looked at her with honest, open eyes, as if he really wanted to know her. *Please put him on my team, Max!* she silently prayed.

"I'm Shane," she said, introducing herself.

"Funky name," Adam said. "I like it."

"Yeah, my father had a thing for old Westerns," she explained. "It's the name of the hero in one of my dad's favorite films."

"Lucky he didn't name you Trigger," Adam joked, and the dimples popped up again.

Cute, Shane thought. *Totally cute!*

The girl with the serious attitude stuck out her hand. "I'm Kelly Turman," she announced. "But my friends call me The Terminator. I'm a competitive swimmer and climber."

"I hear you're just plain competitive," Adam said.

"Okay, that's true," Kelly admitted. "I mean, I'm going for Princeton next year. But Yale's my safety school."

The quietest kid in the bunch was a tall, African American guy with glasses.

"I'm Charles P. Benjamin," he said, shaking hands all around. He explained that he wanted to be a psychiatrist.

"So where's number eight?" Adam asked, looking around. "Isn't someone missing?"

The intern, who had been hanging around at the edge of the group, spoke up. "She'll be here soon," he said. "But right now it's time for your first Campfire Council, where you'll find out who will be your teammates, and who will be your enemies for . . ."

"*The Challenge!*" all the Warriors said at once.

"Take your places, Warriors," Max said, "and let me explain the rules. Two teams. One house. Seven challenges, seven carved wooden statues, or totems. For each event the winning team secures a totem as the prize. At the end of the week, the team with the most totems is the winner of . . . *The Challenge*."

Right on cue, the tiki torches flared up when he said the name of the show.

"Now for the rules," Max went on as Big Joe and two other cameramen circled the campfire.

"Curfew is 10:00 P.M. *No* dating or romantic relationships allowed. Anyone who breaks that rule will be disqualified from an event, which means your team will be at a severe disadvantage. Understood?"

Shane's heart sank, and her eyes caught Adam's again. He looked as disappointed as she felt.

"Tonight we will break you up into two teams," Max went on, "the Aztecs and the Mayans. As your name is called, you will rise, light your Torch of Conflict from the Ceremonial Fire of Competition, and stand near the totem that represents your team." Max reached into the head of a large totem near him and pulled out a slip of paper. "And the first member of Team Aztec is . . . Kelly!"

Kelly rose as if she were about to be crowned Queen of the Jungle. With her head held high, she dipped her torch into the bonfire and lit it. Then she placed it in a torch holder at the outer edge of the circle, near the totem that represented the Aztec team.

Max drew the names one by one. The teams shaped up slowly, and Shane held her breath, hoping she'd be put on a team with Adam. But no such luck.

Let's see, Shane thought. *It's Kelly the Terminator, JJ the performer, Charles the shy guy, and Adam the hottie on the Aztec team. Justin the surfer dude, Anthony the cook, and I are the Mayans.*

"We're still missing someone," Shane whispered, glancing around and wondering where the eighth Warrior was.

"And finally . . ." Max said with a sneaky grin spreading across his face, "our last warrior. . . ."

Where is she? Shane wondered. Then she saw a girl hurrying down the path toward the campfire. Her long blond hair was flying in the ocean breeze.

"Sorry I'm late! I'm never late!" the girl called as she ran to join them.

Shane's mouth fell open in disbelief. No way. This wasn't happening. A lump formed in her throat.

"Meet Lizzie Dalton!" Max announced as Shane's sister stumbled into the circle. "Warrior number eight!"

CHAPTER TWO

"Shane?" Lizzie stared at her twin sister sitting in the Campfire Council. How could this have happened? How could Shane be a competitor on *The Challenge* without Lizzie's knowing about it?

Her mind raced with a zillion questions and possibilities. Did her dad know Shane was going to be on the show? Did their mom?

Shane stepped forward. "What are you doing here?" she said with an accusing look on her face.

"Me? What are *you* doing here?" Lizzie shot back, glaring at Shane, then at Max, then at Shane again.

"Now, girls," Max said. "It just so happens that you were both lucky enough to get on the show. What's the problem?"

"'What's the problem?'" Lizzie repeated. "Just the fact that we can't *stand* each other!" She blurted it out before she noticed that the camera guy was closing in on her, taping.

Great, she thought. *I'm coming off like a world-class witch on national TV.* Her heart started pounding, and she fumbled in her leather bag for her cell phone.

"What are you doing?" Shane demanded.

"I'm calling a cab," Lizzie muttered. "I've got to get out of here."

"Typical," Shane said. "You haven't changed a bit. You can't *function* without your cell phone."

Don't even answer that, Lizzie told herself as she punched the buttons on her cell. She pressed the phone to her ear, praying it would ring. But she couldn't get a signal. "Perfect!" she said. "I'm stuck in the middle of nowhere with you."

Shane threw her hands up. "Don't worry, I'm out of here. I quit!"

"You can't quit," Lizzie argued, "because I'm going to quit. I'm gone."

"Fine," Shane said. "Then I'll stay. No sense in both of us quitting."

Wait a minute, Lizzie thought. *Did Shane just trick me into quitting so she could stay?* Lizzie narrowed her eyes. "Hang on," she said. "I've changed my mind. I'm not quitting."

"Well, neither am I," Shane announced, standing her ground.

"Okay, good," Max said, beaming and glancing over at the cameraman. "You get all that?"

The cameraman nodded. "Got it."

Max introduced Lizzie to the cast and crew. "Take a few minutes to get to know everyone," he told her. "Then we'll all go to the bungalow and you'll see your rooms."

Lizzie's head was swimming, but she had to put her feelings about Shane aside if she was going to win a scholarship. And it wasn't hard to figure out who the prime competition was. Kelly had do-or-die written all over her.

Lizzie pulled out her Palm Pilot and jotted down a few notes about the other team. Then she glanced up and spotted the cutest guy she'd seen in months. He seemed to be around her age, but from the clipboard in his hands, she could tell he was working for the show.

"Hi," the guy said, grinning at the Palm Pilot she was holding. "I'm Marcus. You like to stay organized, huh?"

"Hi." Lizzie stuffed the Palm back into her bag. "I guess you could say that."

Marcus tapped his back pocket. "I don't go anywhere without mine either."

"Seriously?" Lizzie was surprised. Most guys her age were incapable of organizing anything. Half the time they couldn't even organize what to have for lunch.

"It's part of the job," Marcus explained. "You've got to keep it together when you work in television."

"Yeah," Lizzie said, nodding. "I'll bet. Well, if you're so together, what's on the schedule for tonight?"

"Let me answer that," Max Trevor said, standing

nearby. He raised his voice so everyone would listen. "Warriors, tonight you'll be treated to dinner and a night on the town. This is your chance to get to know your friends . . . and your enemies."

I already know my number-one enemy, Lizzie thought sadly, glancing at Shane.

Shane caught her eye, and for a minute Lizzie almost thought her sister looked upset, too. But then Shane went back to talking to Adam.

Okay, be that way, Lizzie thought. *We don't have to speak to each other. We just have to make sure we win the scholarships.*

Everyone seemed excited as Marcus led the group toward the resort bungalow where they were going to live for the week. "This is your room," he said, opening the door for Lizzie and Shane. "I made sure you got a room overlooking the pool."

"Nice," Lizzie said, checking out the balcony and the view.

"See you tonight," Marcus called as he led the other Warriors to their rooms.

Lizzie hauled her duffel bag into the room and quickly dropped it on the best bed.

Shane immediately started spreading her candles and crystals all over the place. "Why do *you* get the bed near the window?" she complained.

"I want fresh air," Lizzie replied.

"Why?" Shane asked. "Just for the novelty of it?

I mean, you live in an apartment with the windows sealed and the air-conditioning blasting all the time."

"How would *you* know if the windows are closed?" Lizzie asked. "You haven't been there in two years."

"So? You could have come to L.A.," Shane replied. "Airplanes fly both ways, you know."

I'm not going to argue, Lizzie decided. *Why stoop to Shane's level? I tried calling her last year, and she never called me back.*

Lizzie unzipped her bag and carried some tank tops to the rattan dresser. But just then she spotted a large spider crawling across the floor. "Ewww!" She dropped her clothes and reached for a shoe.

"What?" Shane asked. "What's wrong?"

"A spider!" Lizzie cried, about to pound the thing to dust.

"Nooooo!" Shane screamed. She threw herself in front of the spider and spread her arms wide. "Don't! He has just as much right to live as you do!"

"*He*?" Lizzie said. "It's not a *he*. It's an *it*!"

"So I guess you'll mow down any living thing that gets in your way," Shane accused her.

Is that really what she thinks of me? Lizzie wondered.

Someone knocked on the bedroom door. Lizzie marched over to it and flung it open. Anthony and

Justin, their two teammates, were standing outside.

"Uh, could you guys keep it down in there?" Anthony asked. "We can hear you two fighting all over the house."

"That sibling stuff is whack, yo," Justin added.

"Sorry," Lizzie said, embarrassed. It wasn't usually her style to argue, let alone in front of people.

She saw Kelly laughing behind the two guys. "Hey!" Kelly said. "Keep it up, girls! That's the sound of my college scholarship coming from your room!"

Lizzie closed the door and finished unpacking. Shane had picked up the spider and put it out the window. Now she was sitting cross-legged on her bed, meditating or something.

For any other sisters this experience might actually be fun, Lizzie thought. *Too bad it won't turn out that way for us.*

She pulled a book from her duffel. It was the one thing she really thought she'd need to win on this show—her *Worst Possible Situations Handbook*.

I wonder if there's a chapter on reuniting with a sister who hates you, Lizzie said to herself. *Because surviving* The Challenge *is going to be a way bigger challenge than I'd thought!*

CHAPTER THREE

"You're wearing *that* to dinner?" Lizzie asked Shane later that evening. She couldn't help it. The jeans and paisley peasant blouse Shane had on just didn't make it for a night out on the town.

"Don't you think *you're* a little over the top?" Shane shot back, staring at the slinky black dress Lizzie had slipped into.

"We'll have plenty of time to get down and dirty in the next few days," Lizzie argued. *Besides, I want to look nice in front of Marcus*, she thought, heading for the door.

The other contestants were waiting for them in the living room. JJ was wearing a satin dress. Her hair was up in an elaborate twist with red rhinestone pins stuck in everywhere.

"See?" Lizzie whispered. "I'm not overdressed At least not compared to *her*!"

Marcus hung near the doorway in a pair of khakis and a white shirt. "Okay, everyone's here," he announced, smiling directly at Lizzie. "Let's go."

A shuttle bus took them from the resort to a restaurant in town. Inside, colorful lanterns hung from the rafters. Mariachi music played on the sound system.

Lizzie sat near the end of a long wooden table. Marcus quickly took the seat next to her.

This is going well already! Lizzie thought, picking up a menu from the table.

Then Shane sat down across from her, with Adam at her side.

Several minutes later a waiter came to take their orders.

"I'll have a green salad and a side of rice and beans," Shane told him.

Of course she will, Lizzie thought, rolling her eyes.

"Rice and beans for me, too," Adam said, grinning at Shane.

Shane's face lit up. "Are you a vegetarian?"

Adam shrugged. "Ever since I did an article on the meat-packing industry I haven't been able to touch the stuff."

Lizzie stuck her chin into the air and made eye contact with the waiter. "I'll have a steak. Rare."

"Why do you always have to make a big deal out of being a cow-eater?" Shane asked.

"I'm not making a big deal," Lizzie argued, although she knew that wasn't exactly true. And she couldn't help feeling a pang inside. This was the first meal she'd had with her sister in two years. Why did things have to start out this way? Why did she let Shane push her buttons so that every conversation turned into a battle?

"You okay?" Marcus asked, staring into her eyes.

"Sure," Lizzie said. "Just thinking."

Marcus nodded, then glanced down the length of the table, to the far end. Kelly and Charles were arm wrestling. Kelly seemed to be winning. "What are they doing?" he asked.

"Arm wrestling to see who gets to be team captain," Anthony explained.

"Wait a minute," JJ said. "How can you have a team captain in a talent contest?"

"*The Challenge* isn't about talent," Anthony said. "It's about daring tests of endurance and knowledge."

JJ gasped. "Are you joking?" She looked horrified. "I thought we were competing for a record deal!"

Lizzie and half the people at the table burst out laughing.

Then Lizzie reached for a tortilla chip and some salsa. She tried not to eavesdrop, but she couldn't help hearing what Shane and Adam were talking about.

"Tell me," Shane was saying, "why journalism?"

"I want to be where the action is," Adam said. "There's so much to see and write about. What about you? Why Earth science?"

"That's easy. You want to *see* the world," Shane answered. "I want to *save* it."

Adam tilted his head and smiled. "Something tells me you'll do it, too."

"I don't know," Shane said with a laugh. "Last

year I was tree-sitting to protect old-growth forests from loggers . . ."

"That's where you climb up in a tree and won't come down, so the loggers can't cut it, right?" Adam asked.

"Right," Shane said. "So, I was up about forty feet when my head started spinning. Turns out I have vertigo."

Wow, Lizzie thought, listening. *That must have been scary.*

"Really? You get dizzy when you're up high?" Adam looked concerned. "Let's hope there's no rock climbing or high diving on the show."

"Hey, Adam. You're on *our* team. She's on *their* team," Kelly pointed out. "Let's hope there *is*!"

"Kelly never lets up, does she?" Lizzie asked Marcus.

"Not that I've seen," he admitted.

"I suppose I should wish she were on my team," Lizzie said. "But, I'm glad they're stuck with her."

"She's pretty tough," Marcus said. "You think you can whip her on *The Challenge*?"

"As long as the events don't involve snakes," Lizzie admitted. "That's the only thing I can't handle."

Marcus smiled at her and nodded toward the small dance floor. The mariachis had stopped playing, and pulsing latin rhythms were now blaring from the sound system. "Want to dance?"

"Okay," Lizzie said.

Marcus took her by the arm, and she followed him to the dance floor. He was so confident—so much more in control of his life than a lot of the guys who went to her school.

"How did you get a job on *The Challenge* anyway?" Lizzie asked, shouting to be heard above the music.

"I got the internship through UCLA. I'll be starting there in the fall," Marcus said. "So what are you all about, Lizzie? Wait. Don't tell me. I'm good at reading people."

"You really think you can?" Lizzie asked, challenging him.

"Hmm." Marcus tilted his head to one side and eyed her carefully. "Okay, here's my take on you. You're senior class president. You never go anywhere without your cell phone and Palm Pilot. You'll eat anything as long as it's ordered in. You volunteered to work on a senator's campaign, and after Georgetown you've got your eye on law school. You figure you'll work on Capitol Hill for a while, then run for office yourself."

Lizzie stopped dancing and stared at him with her mouth open. "Wow. You're good," she said. "How'd you do that?"

"I saw your audition tape," Marcus admitted with a laugh.

"Ooh!" Lizzie said, playfully hitting him on the

arm. Still, the thought of those audition tapes made her frown.

"What's wrong?" Marcus asked above the music.

"Nothing," Lizzie said. "But if I ever get my hands on the weasel who decided to put my sister and me on the show together, I'll strangle him. It's just so low, don't you think?"

"I don't know," Marcus said slowly. "I mean, that's what these reality shows are all about—conflict. Right?"

"I guess," Lizzie said with a shrug. "And I know you work for the show, so you have to defend those slimeballs. But you're not really one of them, right?"

"No way," Marcus said. He quickly looked away. Then he reached down and felt his pocket. "Sorry. Cell phone's vibrating. I've got to take this." He stopped dancing and excused himself, heading outside where it was quieter.

"Too bad UCLA isn't on the East Coast," Lizzie mumbled as she watched him walk away. "Or I wouldn't mind going there myself. . . ."

"Marcus? It's Max," the voice on the cell phone said. "Did you get anything we can use to spice up the show yet?"

Marcus closed his eyes and took a deep breath. *I don't want to do this*, he thought. *Lizzie is so nice. And so is Shane.*

23

He had no idea when he proposed this sisters-who-hate-each-other idea that he was going to start falling for one of them, practically on the first day.

"Well," Max said. "Are you going to tell me what you learned?"

Yeah, Marcus thought. *I figured out that the Dalton sisters are nice girls who seem to have a lot of strong feelings for each other under the surface. And they don't deserve to have their emotions played with.*

"Marcus, either you work for me here—or you don't work on the show," Max said in an all-business tone of voice. "And don't forget—I've got a big bonus for you if you come through."

"Okay, okay," Marcus blurted out. "Shane is afraid of heights, and Lizzie's afraid of snakes."

"Fantastic," Max said. "I'm sure we can use that somewhere."

"Listen, I'm not really comfortable doing this," Marcus tried to explain.

"Kid, *you* wanted this job in entertainment," Max said, "and sisters who get along . . . *not* entertaining. Now get back to work."

"Yeah," Marcus said, hanging up. "Back to my job—as a slimeball."

CHAPTER FOUR

"At least Max had the good sense to put me in the lead," Lizzie said as she led the other Mayans toward the first challenge.

"Give me a break," Shane muttered. Just because Lizzie was walking ahead didn't mean she was in charge! "You're only in the lead because we're going that way," she added. *"I'm* in the lead if we turn around and head back to the resort."

The Mayans stumbled toward a bamboo structure on the beach. Lizzie was first, then Justin, Anthony, and Shane. They were all wearing flippers on their feet.

Ahead, Shane saw that the Aztec team was already waiting for them. They were wearing flippers, too. Kelly was at one end, JJ at the other. Adam and Charles were in the middle.

Max and the rest of the camera crew stood near the water. "Warriors, welcome to Day One of . . . *The Challenge!*" Max pointed to the bamboo structure. "We call this the Labyrinth. Mayans, your entrance is on the left. Aztecs, on the right."

The two teams moved toward their openings to the maze.

"At the center of this maze is a wooden totem," Max went on. "First team to capture it wins." He walked up to the maze with two maps in his hands. "You have ten seconds to study the map. When you hear the sound of the conch shell being blown, drop the maps and go!"

He handed one map to the Aztecs. Kelly grabbed it and started studying. Lizzie grabbed for the other.

"Your ten seconds begin . . . now!" Max cried.

"Let me see that. You're terrible with maps," Shane said quickly, reaching for the paper.

"At least I don't navigate using the planets and crystals!" Lizzie snapped, holding on tightly.

"Just let me see it," Shane said, "or we're going to lose!" She reached for one side of the map and pulled.

Lizzie held on to the other side. All at once the map ripped in two. "Good going," she said, glaring at Shane.

"Time's up!" Max called as the conch sounded.

"Let's go!" Shane said, leading her team into the maze. Big Joe and another cameraman followed them.

"Which way?" Justin said. "You girls are the only ones who saw the map."

Shane glanced from side to side. She thought she remembered how the path went. "This way." She dragged her team to the left.

"No," Lizzie insisted. "We go right and *then* left."

She tried to pull them to the right and around a tight corner. Justin and Anthony started to follow her.

"No, I'm telling you, it's this way!" Shane pulled as hard as she could, and Anthony and Justin tumbled toward her.

"Ow!" Anthony cried, rubbing his wrists.

"Yo, ladies," Justin said.

"Okay, stop!" Shane said. "Look, Lizzie, I know what I'm saying. We need to go to the left!"

"All those veggie burgers have clogged your brain," Lizzie snapped.

"Me? You'd get lost going from the beach to the ocean!" Shane said.

"This is whack, yo," Justin said. "Look . . ." He pointed to the other side of the bamboo fence.

The Aztecs were in lockstep, with Kelly leading the way. "Left! Over! Right! Under!" she shouted. "Follow me!"

"Come on, dude-ettes," Justin said. "Do me a solid and pick a direction, okay?"

Fine, Shane thought. She headed to the left, and the rest of them followed her. But around the corner they came to a bamboo pole they had to climb over. Or go under.

Shane hesitated, and Lizzie lunged forward, trying to get into the lead. Within seconds the four of them were hopelessly tangled up with the pole.

"We won!" Kelly cried from the middle of the maze.

"Aztecs rule!" the other voices shouted and cheered.

The Mayans had lost the first event.

"All right, teams." Max motioned for them to follow him to the next competition. "I have a real *treat* for you in this next challenge," he said with a devilish smirk.

"I don't like this guy," Anthony mumbled. "He's having *way* too much fun watching us sweat."

Shane nodded as they hurried from the picnic table where they'd been eating to a remote spot on the beach. She had a feeling that this event wouldn't be much of a "treat."

"After one event Team Aztec leads with one totem to none," Max announced to the cameras. "Our next event is one of my favorites. It's called . . . Don't Spill the Beans." Max snickered and looked up at a huge iron pot that was suspended high overhead from a large wooden structure. Two ropes were attached to either side of the pot. Two production assistants held on to each rope.

"Aztecs, Mayans, line up here," Max said, pointing to two spots under the bucket. "This event is simple. Above you is a bucket full of soupy black beans. In my hand are questions for each team." He waved a blue index card. "Answer a question right in ten seconds or less, and the bucket will lean toward the other team. Answer it wrong, it tips toward you. In the end the clean team wins." He paused dramatically to stare at both teams. "Okay, question one is for the Aztecs. Who created Spider-man?"

Kelly and her teammates huddled up fast. They all seemed to agree.

"Stan Lee and Steve Ditko," Adam answered.

"Correct!" Max announced.

Yikes, Shane thought. She gazed up at the bucket. It tipped a little in their direction.

"Mayans," Max said. "What is the capital of Switzerland?"

Shane leaned in so they could huddle.

"Geneva?" Lizzie said.

"Interlaken," Shane said.

"I'm almost positive it's Geneva," Lizzie replied.

"Listen, it's—" Justin tried to get a word in.

"Three seconds," Max warned them.

Maybe Lizzie's right, Shane decided. "Geneva!" she blurted out as their official answer.

"Interlaken!" Lizzie cried at the same time.

"Sorry," Max said. "Bern is the capital of Switzerland."

"Man, you Bobbseys are going to wipe out our chances to hang up on the backside air and then pull it," Justin complained.

"What does that mean?" Lizzie asked.

Who cares? Shane thought, gazing up again at the bean pot. *We're going to get splattered!*

"Next question to the Aztecs," Max said with a twinkle in his eye. "What's the former name of Istanbul?"

"Constantinople!" Kelly shouted out.

"Correct!" Max called.

Adam rolled his eyes. "Hey, Kel, maybe next time we can at least *pretend* to huddle. You know?"

Justin looked up at the tipping bean bucket. "Whoa."

"One more wrong answer may send the Mayans to the showers," Max said in his most dramatic television voice. Big Joe circled around them, aiming the camera at Lizzie, then Shane.

"Okay, Mayans," Max said. "You have to get this question right. What is the largest department store in the world?"

"This one's all yours, girls," Anthony said.

"Macys," Shane replied fast.

"No, it's Bloomingdale's," Lizzie said in a voice that sounded as if she wanted to add *you idiot*.

"No, it's got to be Macys," Shane insisted.

"*No*, it's definitely Bloomie's," Lizzie said firmly.

"Macys!" Shane shouted.

"Bloomie's!" Lizzie shouted back.

"Sorry, time's up!" Max shouted. "The answer is: Macys," Max announced.

Before Shane could even cover her head with her hands, the bucket tilted again. The beans poured out, covering them with gooey, wet black slime.

Kelly and JJ burst out laughing. Charles snorted, and even Adam chuckled. But then his eyes met Shane's, and he gave her a sympathetic smile.

"Gross," Lizzie said, wiping beans from her hair and face.

"Look on the bright side," Shane said, trying to put a positive spin on the whole thing. "At least it's vegetarian."

"Give me a break," Anthony muttered. "They don't even care that they totally messed up."

Big Joe hovered beside them, taping every word they said.

Justin shook his head, turned, and walked away.

Shane instantly felt awful. *Uh-oh*, she thought, glancing at Lizzie. *Those guys blame us for losing— and they're right!*

CHAPTER FIVE

The moon was just a sliver in the sky that night as the Mayans and the Aztecs marched down to the beach from the bungalow for the Campfire Council.

"Welcome," Max said as Big Joe and two other cameramen circled the fire. "Have a seat." He gestured grandly, playing up the role of host. "Today's score: Aztecs, two. Mayans, nothing. Zero, zip, zilch, *la grande nada* . . ."

"We got it, Max," Lizzie said.

Max handed a second totem to Kelly, who had the first one resting in her lap. "As you know, the winner for each day receives a reward," he said. "What you don't know—since I just added this little twist—is that the loser receives a punishment."

Punishment? Shane wondered what it could be.

"Tonight the Aztecs will dine on a catered meal. Afterward they'll spend time in the hot tub and listen to music while sipping cool drinks," Max said.

"Yes!" Kelly shouted, shooting a fist into the air.

"Meanwhile," Max went on, "the Mayans will be pitching tents on the beach and eating a dinner of franks and beans."

"More beans?" Shane mumbled.

"At least it's vegetarian," Lizzie, Justin, and Anthony all said at the same time.

Shane covered her face with her hands. *How many times are they going to make that joke today?* she wondered. *Twenty? Thirty?*

When the Campfire Council was over, Marcus appeared with a load of camping gear. "Sorry, but you're on your own from here," he said, shooting Lizzie a look that said *I wish I could stay and help*.

Hmm, Shane thought. *Lizzie and Marcus? Yeah, that made sense.*

"Have a good night," Marcus said, his eyes locked on Lizzie's.

"Thanks," she said, sounding as if she totally doubted that would happen.

The Mayans hauled the gear down to the beach and started pitching their individual tents. A camera crew followed them. Within minutes Justin and Anthony had their tents up.

Shane pitched hers easily, too. "My mom and I go camping all the time," she explained to the guys.

But Lizzie just stood there, staring.

"What's the matter with her?" Anthony asked Shane.

"She's not the outdoorsy type," Shane explained.

"Too bad," Justin said, lying back on his sleeping bag and gazing up at the stars. "Check out those light blasts."

For a few minutes Lizzie struggled to put up her

tent. But it wasn't happening. She didn't seem to know which side was the top! Finally she reached into her backpack and pulled out a book and a small flashlight.

"You're going to read?" Justin asked.

"So?" Lizzie said. "I'm taking a break."

Shane glanced up and saw that Lizzie was reading her *Worst Possible Situations Handbook. I kind of feel sorry for her,* she thought. *If Lizzie doesn't get that tent up, she's going to be really cold tonight. The temperature is dropping already. Besides, we* said *we needed to work together for the sake of the team.*

"You want some help?" Shane offered softly, getting up and moving toward her sister.

Lizzie glanced at Big Joe, who was filming the whole thing. "No thanks. I can handle it," she said, too proud to give in.

Shane backed away. "Okay, have it your way. I was just trying to help."

Lizzie closed the book and struggled to get her tent up again. But just then a huge wave crashed onto the shore. The water washed up to the spot where her tent was and carried it out into the ocean.

"Arrgh!" Lizzie cried out in frustration. She looked right into the camera. "I hate nature!"

Shane stifled a laugh. "Hey, you can't say I didn't try," she said.

• • •

"Now feel the stretch," Shane said as she stood on the beach the next morning, leading her team in yoga exercises. Well, minus Lizzie, anyway.

She, Justin, and Anthony all had their eyes closed as they stood on one leg with the other extended out in front of them.

"Find your *ujjai* breath," Shane said. "It's a special kind of breathing. It makes a sound in your throat when you exhale." She heard a weird gurgling sound coming from both guys. *Not quite*, she thought. *But at least they're trying!*

"Can I join?" asked a voice from behind her.

Shane opened her eyes and saw Adam standing there, wearing shorts and a T-shirt.

"Sure," she said. "But aren't you supposed to be hanging with your group?"

Adam nodded toward the far end of the beach, where Kelly was leading her team in military-style jumping jacks. "This looks like more fun."

Shane smiled. "Okay. Just follow along." She turned back to Anthony and Justin, who were each wobbling on one leg. "Lower your hands to your heart and then move to Downward Dog."

"And you think *I* don't speak English?" Justin said.

"Shh," Shane said. "Breathe slowly. Find your inner *chi*." Out of the corner of her eye Shane could see a cameraman taping them. She tried to ignore him, but it was hard to stay focused with someone filming her. From down the beach she heard Kelly's team marching and shouting army chants.

"Are you sure this inner *chi* thing is going to beat their boot-camp thing?" Justin asked.

Shane nodded calmly. "It's all about the *chi*."

"Adam!" Kelly shouted. "Get your butt back here and give me fifty push-ups!"

"The sarge is calling me. Gotta go!" Adam gave a salute, then hurried back to his own team.

Shane laughed, then spotted Lizzie walking toward them with a cardboard tray holding four cups of coffee.

"Okay, people, I've got caffeine," Lizzie said as if that were the solution to all their problems.

"We're doing yoga," Anthony said, still balancing.

"Nice," Lizzie said, "if freezing on the beach last night wasn't enough. The other team's got the Terminator and I've got Yogi and her two Boo-Boos."

Typical, Shane thought. *She makes fun of it because she doesn't understand it.* "Have you got a better idea, Lizzie?"

"Yes," Lizzie said, approaching the group. "We should be studying the *Worst Possible Situations Handbook*. You know, things like what to do if your tongue gets stuck on a block of ice. Or how to survive an elephant stampede! Not all this junk."

"Good thinking!" Shane said, rolling her eyes. "I just saw that elephant over by the pool, and I'm pretty sure he was standing on a big block of ice. . . ."

"Yo, sibs!" Justin shouted. "Enough with the aggro!"

"Justin's right," Anthony said. "It's time you ladies got over yourselves. We're losing because you're fighting."

Shane gulped and glanced at Lizzie. "He's got a point," she said softly.

"I guess," Lizzie admitted.

Shane faced her sister. "Look. Do you want to declare a cease-fire? Because how else are we going to win—"

"*The Challenge!*" Justin and Anthony both cried out at once.

"Sorry," Anthony added. "It just came out."

Shane waited for Lizzie to say something. Anything. Hello?

Finally Lizzie nodded solemnly. "Okay. We put our personal issues on the shelf. And we work together as a team."

"Sure. For the sake of the team," Shane said. "But I don't want to hear another vegetarian bean joke as long as I'm here. Got that?"

"Deal." Lizzie almost smiled but then she stopped herself.

I'll take what I can get, Shane thought.

CHAPTER SIX

An hour later Max called the two teams to an event held in a clearing in the woods. Once there the Warriors found a large wooden turntable with eight compartments—each one filled with something gross to eat.

"This event is called You Are What You Eat. We have quite a buffet," Max said, pointing dramatically to the display of horrible foods. "Jalapeno peppers, snake meat, cat food, worms, raw liver, a raw egg, some tasty cockroaches, and, of course . . . the dreaded Christmas fruitcake!"

Everyone laughed when he identified the last item.

"Spin the wheel and eat the food that lands in front of you. Your team gets a point for each thing you eat completely," Max said, unable to hide his delight. "And you've *got* to keep it down."

"You're just loving this, aren't you?" Lizzie said.

"I like my job," Max admitted with a smug smile. "Let's see how much you like *yours*. Adam, you go first."

Adam leaned forward and spun the turntable. "Show me the fruitcake!" The turntable slowed to a stop. A cup with a raw egg landed in front of him.

"No problem," Adam said. He lifted the cup to his lips, squeezed his eyes shut, and drank the egg. He sort of gulped and gagged as it went down.

"Whoa," Max said as the camera crew came in for a close-up. "That one almost came back up." He grinned. "It's one point for the Aztecs. Lizzie, it's your turn next."

Lizzie reached forward and gave the wheel a good push. "Fruitcake!" she prayed. "Please, fruit-cake!" The wheel stopped on something lumpy, a light-brownish color.

"Snake meat!" Max announced. "Raw. And you've got to swallow that entire slimy chunk to score a point for your team."

Lizzie shuddered. Snakes! She hated them. But at least this one was dead.

"You can do it," Shane said.

Wow, Lizzie thought. *Is that really my sister cheering for me?* She put on her game face and popped the snake meat into her mouth and chewed. It was so cold and slimy that it made her want to gag. But finally she swallowed it. She took a few quick deep breaths to keep herself from spewing.

"We scored!" Shane yelled, jumping up and down. She was so excited, she almost reached out and hugged Lizzie.

"Big deal." Kelly sneered.

The next to spin was Charles. He got the raw

liver. He winced and gagged but managed to keep it down. Then Justin spun and got cockroaches. He ate them without even flinching.

"Kelly, your turn," Max said.

Kelly spun the wheel and got jalapeno peppers. Her face turned red after the first bite, but she handled it.

"That brings us to our sixth player," Max said. "Our vegetarian, Shane. Ooh, you wouldn't want to eat *meat*, would you?" He chuckled.

"Let's just do it." Shane took a deep breath.

Everyone watched Shane closely as she stepped up and gave the turntable a shove. As the wheel slowed in front of her, she closed her eyes tightly.

"Earthworms!" Max announced gleefully.

"No!" Shane's hands flew up to cover her mouth.

"Don't worry. They probably taste like chicken," Anthony said.

"But I don't *eat* chicken!" Shane replied, horrified. "How many do I have to eat?" she asked Max.

"Just one," he said. "Since it's still *alive*!"

Shane gagged at the thought. She picked up a worm between two fingers and almost heaved.

"You can do it!" Anthony cheered.

"Yeah!" Lizzie chimed in. "Just go for it!"

Shane closed her eyes, opened her mouth wide, and ate it. For half a second it seemed as if she was going to puke. Shane forced herself to swallow. Hard.

"You did it! We're tied!" Anthony cheered.

Lizzie and the other Mayans raced up to congratulate her.

"Thanks, you guys," Shane said, looking kind of sick. "You pulled me through this."

JJ was up next. She spun the wheel and got cat food. She stepped right up, took three forkfuls, and munched as if it were a low-calorie appetizer.

Lizzie stared at her, amazed.

"What?" JJ said, shrugging it off. "It tastes like tuna."

"Remind me never to eat at your house," Adam joked.

"Anthony, it's all up to you," Max announced. "The score right now is Aztecs, four, Mayans, three. If you score a point, we'll go to a tiebreaker. Otherwise, the Aztecs win."

"Okay, Ma," Anthony said, looking right into the camera. "You always said I could eat a horse, right?"

Then he spun the wheel. It stopped on fruitcake.

"Yes!" Lizzie and the other Mayans cheered.

"Noooo!" Anthony said, backing away.

"What? You've got a problem with fruitcake?" Lizzie couldn't believe it.

"Christmas, 1996. It's a long story." Anthony shook his shoulders to get himself in gear. But the minute he took his first bite of fruitcake, he turned green.

"Uh-oh," Lizzie said. "Looks like he's going to lose it."

"Deep breaths!" Shane urged him. "If I can eat a worm, you can handle a few cherries and raisins."

"Shh!" Anthony mumbled. "Don't mention the ingredients."

"You must swallow it all," Max said, "for a tie."

Anthony tried to chew. But he couldn't do it. "Bllurghhh."

"Dude, you gonna blow some chunkage?" Justin backed up.

Lizzie jumped back, too. Just in time. Two seconds later Anthony lost most of the fruitcake he'd eaten.

"We won!" Kelly screamed, jumping up and down. "We won!"

"Excellent!" Max said, grinning from ear to ear. He turned to Big Joe. "I love this! Barfing is great for the ratings!"

Lizzie frowned at Max. *I wonder if drop-kicking a host is good for ratings*, she thought.

"First they force-feed us worms, then offer us lunch?" Shane said. "How sick is that?"

Adam laughed. "Maybe Max is trying to save money," he joked. "He figures we won't eat a bite after all that barfing."

It was later that afternoon and Shane and Adam were chilling out, finishing off a catered box lunch on the beach. The two of them had managed to sit together without making it seem obvious that they liked each other.

I still wish Adam was on my team, Shane thought. *The way things are, all the Aztecs hang out together and all the Mayans hang out together. The two almost never mix.*

"All right, teams," Max called. "Let's go. The next event is waiting for you."

Shane and the others jumped up and followed Max to a clearing in the trees. There were two separate pens of farm animals waiting for them, side by side.

"Now this is my kind of event," Shane said. "I love animals—as long as they're still moving and not on my plate."

Max stepped between the two teams and stared into the camera Big Joe was holding. "We like to call this challenge Animal Farm." Max showed them how each of the smaller pens opened into a larger pen in the middle. "The first team to get all your animals into the big pen wins," he explained. "Be careful not to hurt them. Warriors, take your marks. Ready, set . . ."

"Wait!" Lizzie cried. "We don't have a plan!"

The conch shell sounded, and Shane dashed into the pen. *Who needs a plan?* she thought. But all at once a set of sprinklers came on. Water started spraying the whole area.

43

"Hey!" Lizzie cried. "No fair! This place is turning to total mud!"

Shane slipped and almost fell in the muddy pen. "Is there anything Max Trevor won't do for ratings?"

"Come on, Miss Piggy," Justin said, pulling on the front legs of a pig. "Come on. This way."

Anthony pushed the same pig from the back. But the thing wouldn't budge.

"You can't just *push* them," Shane said. "They're not pieces of furniture."

Lizzie grabbed the neck of a goat and tugged. It held its ground. "You stubborn old goat!" she cried. Then she sort of laughed and added, "I bet you get that a lot."

In the other pen the Aztecs were doing the same thing, pulling and pushing the animals while trying not to fall.

This is insane, Shane thought. *These animals aren't going to move. Not with all these bad vibes around them.*

A chicken flapped its wings, and Anthony tried to grab it by the feet.

"Stop!" Shane shouted.

Everyone froze. Lizzie, Anthony, and Justin stared at her.

"What?" Anthony asked, waiting for an explanation.

Shane didn't answer. She closed her eyes and

tried to calm her own breathing. "Find your inner *chi*," she said. "Let's be at peace with the world. Then we can lead the animals to the center of their own Zen experience." She walked to the middle of the pen and began to chant. "Ommmmmmmm . . ."

"She's gone loony," Anthony whispered to Lizzie.

"No, I haven't," Shane said. "I know what I'm doing. In Santa Fe I took a seminar on animal communication."

The goat stood perfectly still, watching Shane intently. It looked as if it was going to follow her.

It took one step toward her, then another. Then it followed her into the center pen!

"Way to go!" Anthony shouted.

"Score one for the Mayans!" Max announced when they had led all the animals into the big pen. "You're still trailing three to one . . . but you're in the game."

"We did it!" Shane cried, and the Mayans celebrated. She glanced over at the Aztecs just in time to see Kelly slip and fall in the mud.

"Each team won an event today," Max said. "We're going to need a tiebreaker to see who gets the reward dinner . . . and who gets the punishment." He led them to another area that was set up with a target and some spears. "In Mayan culture spear-throwing determined who the greatest warriors were. So the first spear thrower to hit the target wins!"

One by one the Mayans and Aztecs took their turns. Shane, Charles, Anthony, Adam, Lizzie, JJ, and Justin all missed.

Then Kelly was up. "'Scuse me," she said, hefting the spear like some kind of crazed Amazon. "A little elbow room, please." She leaned back and put her whole body into it.

"Bull's-eye!" Charles cheered when her spear hit the target.

"All right!" Max said, looking happy that Kelly's team had won. "The Aztecs get the reward! You'll be treated to a steak-and-lobster dinner. And the losers?" he went on. "Well, I'm sorry to tell you, but the Mayans may eat only what they can catch . . . with their bare hands!"

CHAPTER SEVEN

"I think I got something!" Lizzie cried, stabbing her spear into the water that evening. "Come on, dinner!"

"Really? Where?" Justin asked, eyeing her eagerly. "My stomach is growling, man."

Lizzie pulled her spear out of the water. At the end of it was a large clump of kelp. "Oh," she said.

Behind them on the deck near the water, the Aztecs were eating their reward dinner and taunting the Mayans.

"Hey, you guys!" Kelly called to them. "Maybe you'll catch more dinner if you try chanting!"

"Thanks for the tip," Lizzie moaned, stabbing at the water again with no luck. Then she noticed her sister. Shane was on the shore, trying to knock down a coconut from a tree with a rock.

"Ow!" An instant later Big Joe fell to the ground.

"Sorry!" Shane said. "I didn't know you were up there."

"He's everywhere," Anthony called. "No matter where you go, you're never alone."

"I don't care who's watching," Lizzie said. "I just want to catch something to eat!" But all she could see in the water were little minnows and a few jellyfish. "There has to be a better way," Lizzie announced, trudging to shore. She dropped her spear on the beach and headed toward the pool. As she rounded a corner, she ran smack into Marcus.

"Whoa!" Marcus said. He was juggling a tray with a hamburger and soda from the poolside café.

"Sorry," Lizzie said. "I didn't see you. I think I'm blind with hunger."

Marcus glanced at the food in his hands. He tried to hide it behind his back but couldn't manage it. "This is rough, isn't it?" he said softly. "Sometimes I think Max actually *enjoys* torturing you guys."

"*Sometimes?*" Lizzie said.

"You're right," Marcus said. "Sorry about that."

"It's okay." Lizzie sighed. "It's not your fault. Where were you today, anyway? I didn't see you around."

"Why? Did you *miss* me?" Marcus asked.

"You could say that," Lizzie said, flirting back.

"Good." He smiled at her for a minute. "Max sent me on a million errands. I had to go buy the steaks and lobsters for dinner."

Lizzie closed her eyes and moaned. "Don't mention food. I can smell the melted butter all the way over here."

"I . . . I wish I could help," Marcus said, sounding really sorry for her.

Then Lizzie got an idea. "Hey, maybe you *can* help! Toss me your burger."

"What?" Marcus said. "But why? You can't eat it."

"Trust me," Lizzie said, clapping her hands and then holding them open like a catcher's mitt.

"If you say so." Marcus threw the burger to her, and she caught it.

"What did I just do?" Lizzie asked, beaming.

"You caught a hamburger," Marcus said with a shrug. Then a huge smile spread across his face. "Ohhh. I get it. You *caught* a hamburger! With your bare hands!"

"Yes!" Lizzie said, shooting a victory fist into the air. "Quick—go get some more, okay?" She called to her team on the beach. "Justin! Anthony! Shane! Up here!"

Her teammates hurried to the pool, and a moment later they were all "catching" dinner. Big Joe hovered in the background, taping the whole thing.

Shane took one look at the burgers and passed hers back to Marcus. She nibbled at a piece of kelp in her hands.

"Hey, Shane," Lizzie said. "You can eat bread, can't you?" She took the bun and tomato off her burger and held it up for a pass. "Go deep!"

"Thanks!" Shane said, catching them.

"Take ours, too," Justin said. He and Anthony handed Shane their bread and tomatoes.

Lizzie smiled as she watched Justin, Anthony, and Shane share the food. *Cool*, she thought, *we're really starting to act like a team*. "Give it up for teamwork!" she cried. "The Mayans are on their way!"

Lizzie sat facing the ocean later that night, watching the moon shimmer on the dark water. Today had been pretty cool. The teamwork thing was starting to work. And Shane was pretty impressive, the way she had communicated with that goat.

Still, it's not like anything's going to change between us, Lizzie said to herself. *We're here to win scholarships, not put our broken relationship back together*.

She didn't want to think about it anymore, so she pulled out her cell phone. "I have *got* to check my voice mail," she muttered, punching buttons until she got a Mexican operator on the line. "Operator, *por favor*," Lizzie said, wishing she knew more Spanish. But then her phone went dead. "Oh, man." She sighed.

She stood up and headed back to the bungalow, wondering if the phones inside would be any better.

Marcus was just coming out, carrying his clipboard and notes for the show. "Hi," he said, sounding happy to see her.

"Hi," she said. "Thanks for helping us with dinner tonight."

"It was your idea," he said. "You East Coasters can really think on your feet."

"Yeah," Lizzie agreed. Out of the corner of her eye she spotted Big Joe walking toward them with his camera.

"Hey," Marcus said softly. He glanced at Joe, then back at Lizzie. "Meet me behind the banyan tree in five minutes."

"Really?" Lizzie let her eyes lock on his.

Marcus shot her a quick smile and then walked away before Big Joe could catch them on tape.

Cool, Lizzie thought. After all, she had to have *some* fun on this trip, right?

Shane sat in the living room of the bungalow, reading a book on meditation. Not that she could get into a Zen state here with all the stuff that was going on around her.

Justin and Anthony were battling it out on a video game across the room. Charles and Kelly were playing cards with a take-no-prisoners vengeance.

Adam, who was reading quietly in a big stuffed chair nearby, glanced up from his book and shot her a little smile.

That's the fifth time he's done that, Shane thought. *But who's counting?* She smiled back at him, then hid behind her book before Kelly could catch them flirting.

Adam faked a yawn and put down his book. "I'm going outside for some air." He ambled toward the door, glancing at her on the way.

Was that an invitation? Shane wondered. She waited a moment, then stood, pretending to stretch. "I think I'll take a walk."

No one even bothered to look up.

Cool! Shane thought. She strolled toward the door and then slipped out into the starry night. Adam was waiting for her down on the beach.

"Hi," she said, shivering a little from both the night breeze and the excitement.

"Hi," Adam said. "I'm glad you came out."

"Me, too," Shane replied. She glanced over her shoulder to see if anyone was watching. "But do you think we'll get into trouble? I mean, because of the no-dating rule."

"Well," Adam said as they walked beside the water, "if we just *happened* to be out walking at the same time . . ."

"In the same direction . . ." Shane added, giggling.

"Exactly," Adam said. "There's no rule against that."

"Nope." Shane picked up a shell and tossed it into the water.

They strolled along the beach, talking about the show and about their lives back home.

Adam was quiet for a while. Then he said, "Can

I ask you something? How did you and your sister end up living apart?"

"We all used to live in D.C. when our parents were still together," Shane explained. "They split up when we were fifteen." She stopped, not really wanting to go into the details. The whole divorce thing had been pretty painful.

"My parents split up when I was ten," Adam told her. "It was the worst time of my life. I know the drill."

Shane thought for a minute, remembering how it had been. "At first Lizzie and I were still close," she explained. "I mean, we've always been opposites, but we loved each other. Then Mom got a big job opportunity in L.A. It was her dream job, and she couldn't turn it down."

"Makes sense." Adam nodded.

"And I wanted to go with her," Shane said. "I never really *fit* in Washington. It's so intense—not the vibe I want in my life. Anyway, I guess Lizzie never forgave me for leaving. And we just . . . grew apart."

"Oh." Adam nodded again. "So basically your parents got a divorce, and so did you and Lizzie."

"I guess that's one way to look at it," Shane admitted. "The weird thing is, my parents get along great. And they'd do anything to bring the two of us back together." She hung her head, feeling sad about the whole thing all over again.

"Hey." Adam reached out and took her hand. Then he leaned in close and wrapped her into a warm hug.

"What's going on with you two?" a voice from behind them said suddenly.

They jumped, startled, and whirled around.

"Lizzie?" Shane's mouth dropped open. Lizzie and Marcus were right behind her—holding hands!

"What do you think you're doing?" Lizzie asked.

"What do you think *you're* doing?" Shane shot back, staring at Lizzie's hand linked with Marcus's.

Lizzie dropped Marcus's hand fast.

"Guys?" Adam said. "I hate to break up the start of a good family fight, but . . ." He nodded toward the bushes behind Lizzie.

Lizzie, Marcus, and Shane all turned to see what Adam was talking about. A large figure with a camera on his shoulder was hurrying down the path toward them. Right behind him was another man.

"Oh, no!" Marcus said. "We're busted! That's got to be Max and Big Joe!"

CHAPTER EIGHT

Lizzie awoke the next morning in a great mood. Why not? Last night had been excellent. She and Marcus had spent some serious alone time together. Plus they had escaped from Max and Big Joe without getting caught. And now that she and Shane were working together, it seemed as if they might actually have a chance to *win* this game.

At least that's how it seemed in the morning.

But a few hours later, in the middle of the day's challenge, she could hardly remember why she'd felt so optimistic.

"Let me get this straight," Lizzie said to her teammates. "We've been dropped in the middle of the desert, ten miles from anywhere, right?"

"Check," Justin said.

"And we're out of water and nutrition bars?" Lizzie asked.

"Check," Anthony said.

"Out of sunscreen?" Lizzie asked.

"Check," Shane replied, holding up the empty bottle. "But at least we still have the map!"

"Check," Lizzie said, waving it limply. She stared into the distance in silence. So did the others.

Everyone was too hot, too thirsty, and too tired to do anything else.

"I'm starving," Anthony moaned.

"Me, too," Shane said. "And I can't carry these backpacks another foot."

Me neither, Lizzie thought. How insane was Max, anyway? As if being dropped in the middle of the desert wasn't bad enough, the whole thing was even harder because of Max's "little twist." They had to carry college textbooks in their backpacks the whole time! The team that made it back to the resort first with all their books won.

"This is bad," Shane said. "When Max told us this event was called Survival of the Fittest, I didn't realize it meant we might not actually survive!"

"The Aztecs are probably at the pool by now, sipping drinks out of coconuts." Justin moaned.

Lizzie reached into her backpack and pulled out her survival book. "According to the *Worst Possible Situations Handbook*, we can eat cactus and ants and survive just fine."

Anthony stared at her. "Do you know how many ants I'd have to eat to not feel hungry right now?"

Lizzie wanted to say something upbeat to cheer her team, but she couldn't think of anything. And besides, just then a tourist helicopter passed overhead. The noise made it impossible for anyone to hear.

When it disappeared over a hill, Anthony looked

even more miserable. "If we had a helicopter, we'd be home in five minutes," he said.

"Wait a minute!" Lizzie said. "That gives me an idea!" She reached for her backpack, dug around inside, and pulled out a small compact.

Shane rolled her eyes. "Lizzie, do you really think this is a time to worry about shine?"

"I'm not worried about shine," Lizzie said. "I know how to get us out of here!" She bent over a clump of dried grass and angled the compact's mirror to catch the sun's rays. *This has got to work*, Lizzie thought. *According to the* Worst Possible Situations Handbook, *it's supposed to start a fire.*

When the grass didn't burst into flames, Lizzie took off her sunglasses and used the mirror to reflect the light through the lenses onto the grass. Then she tore a blank page out of the handbook and added it to the dried grass.

"It's catching!" Justin cried as the grass smoked, then turned into a tiny blaze.

Within twenty minutes the four of them had built a fire big enough to make some serious smoke. They gathered branches and spelled out *SOS* in giant letters—big enough to be seen from the sky.

When another helicopter appeared, it circled overhead for a moment, then started to land.

"It worked!" Shane shouted, jumping up and down. "We're hitching a ride back to the resort!"

"You're awesome!" Justin gave Lizzie a high five as they climbed into the helicopter.

"That's my sister!" Shane said proudly.

Lizzie beamed with pride. She couldn't believe it. Shane actually sounded glad that they were in the same family. Maybe this whole reality thing wasn't going to turn out so badly after all!

An hour later the Mayans were by the pool at the resort—drinking pineapple coolers out of coconuts!

"We've got another totem," Shane said, raising her drink. "Here's to the Mayans!"

"I can't wait to see Kelly's face when she gets back," Lizzie added.

"Well, look over your shoulder," Anthony said from a raft in the pool, "because here she comes."

"We're here!" Kelly shouted, racing toward the pool. "Now give me that totem!" When she saw Lizzie, Shane, Justin, and Anthony, she stopped dead in her tracks. "What . . . happened?"

"We beat you," Lizzie announced, grinning at the look of total shock on Kelly's face.

Charles and Adam looked really surprised, too. JJ, on the other hand, didn't seem to care. She was way behind them, walking barefoot with her high heels in her hands.

"No way could you beat us," Kelly said. "How did this happen?"

"Skill," Justin said from a lounge chair.

Kelly glared at Lizzie. "You think you're going to win? Think again." She stomped into the bungalow, kicking over a lounge chair as she went.

"I'd hate to be one of *her* enemies," Lizzie said.

"You *are*," Justin said.

Just then Marcus came out of the bungalow. For a second Lizzie thought he was going to run over to congratulate her. But then he noticed Big Joe circling around.

"Uh, nicely done, Mayans," he said to the group.

"Thanks," Lizzie replied, hiding a smile.

"No, really," Marcus insisted. "I'm impressed. I have to congratulate you." He walked over to Lizzie and held out his hand to shake hers.

Weird, Lizzie thought. *He's being so stiff!* Then she saw that he had a small folded piece of paper in his hand. "Oh, uh, yeah," Lizzie said, shaking his hand. "Thanks."

Marcus let his eyes linger on hers for just a second before he turned and walked off.

Lizzie's heart skipped a beat. *A note!* she thought. She giggled to herself, thinking how junior high it was and how much fun at the same time. Then she hurried into the bungalow. She unfolded the note in the bathroom, where she knew for *sure* there were no cameras.

Bring Shane and meet me at the ATV course in an

hour, she read. *Adam and I will be waiting for you.*

A double date with Shane! Lizzie thought. This was a first. She could hardly wait to tell her sister!

Shane stood in front of the mirror, brushing her hair, with Lizzie at her side. The two of them were getting ready to meet Marcus and Adam. Shane leaned her head to the left, using long strokes to get her hair as smooth and silky as possible. Lizzie was doing the exact same thing.

Lizzie noticed it, half laughed, and stopped.

Shane picked up her pale Shimmering Plum lip gloss and leaned in toward the mirror. She puckered up, her arm bent under her chin to get the gloss on just right. Then she glanced at Lizzie, who was leaning in the *exact* same way! Her arm . . . her pucker face . . . "Shimmering Plum?" she asked Lizzie.

Lizzie nodded. "Good color for you," she said with a smile.

"For *us*," Shane agreed. *So this is what it feels like to have a twin sister*, she thought. *I almost forgot!*

Shane slipped on a pair of jeans and some sandals. She tied a beaded anklet around her left ankle.

Lizzie pulled on a pair of cute blue Capri pants with matching blue canvas shoes. She wore a silver bracelet on her wrist.

"Ready?" Shane asked.

Lizzie nodded.

"This is *not* a good idea, you know," Shane reminded her.

"I know." Lizzie paused. "Let's go!"

"Right!" Shane said, and the two of them hurried to meet the guys at the all-terrain vehicle course.

Shane's heart skipped a beat when she saw Adam standing with Marcus in front of two ATVs. They were parked on a sand dune, facing a wide stretch of hilly desert. Adam was wearing a sky-blue polo shirt, cut-off khakis, and sandals. He looked amazing.

"Hi," Marcus said, dangling two sets of keys from one finger. "So . . . who wants to race whom?"

Lizzie grabbed a set and pulled Shane by the arm. "We'll take you guys on." She squinted into the distance. "First one to that cactus patch wins!"

"Do you even know how to drive one of these things?" Shane asked her sister.

"I'll figure it out!" Lizzie said, hopping into the driver's seat.

For the next hour the four of them had an awesome time. First the girls raced the guys. Then Shane and Adam raced Lizzie and Marcus. Adam drove so fast that Shane screamed the whole way.

Finally Shane got behind the wheel with Adam at her side. "Race you to that boulder!" she called to her sister, who was driving the other ATV with Marcus.

Shane roared toward the boulder, then took a

sharp left and zoomed around a hill covered with yucca trees.

"What's up?" Adam asked.

"Shortcut," Shane said with a smile.

Adam laughed. There was no way this was a shortcut to the boulder. "We're going to lose, you know," he said. "They probably think we're just sneaking off to be alone."

"They're probably right," Shane said, pulling up in the shade of the yuccas. She cut the engine, then hopped up to sit on the back of the driver's seat.

Adam joined her, sitting on the back of his seat as well. He fished around in the rear of the ATV for two bottles of water and handed her one.

"You know, when I'm not starving and out of water, this place rocks," Shane said, taking in the desert landscape.

"This place *is* rocks," Adam joked, nodding toward the boulders. "It's one of the wildest places I've ever seen."

"Have you traveled much?" Shane asked.

"Not a lot, but my brother and I always talk about it," Adam said. "After college we're planning to buy Eurail passes and bum around Europe."

"Seeing Europe with your brother," Shane said, thinking about it. Maybe one day she'd be close enough with Lizzie again to do something like that. "That sounds pretty amazing."

It was the first day of the The Challenge competition. My sister, Lizzie, was on my team. We're so different. How were we going to make this work?

I'm a nature-lover,
a vegetarian, and I love yoga.

Lizzie prefers staying in a hotel
to camping out.

But we had to work together. Afterall, the team's college scholarships were at stake!

I had no idea Lizzie was such a team player! She even ate snake meat for the sake of the team!

And she stood on a totem for hours.

Before we
knew it, Lizzie and I were enjoying
spending time together....

And our teamwork paid off....

We won
The Challenge!

It was hard to say good-bye.

A new relationship with my sister
was just beginning!

"Well, I think you're pretty amazing," Adam said, inching closer to her. "Pretty *and* amazing."

Shane blushed. "I'm going to pretend you didn't say that," she said. "Because if you *did*, then I'd have to tell you how amazing I think *you* are. Which I do. And if I said that, then you might move a little closer . . ."

"You mean like this?" Adam scooted close and wrapped his arms around her.

Shane closed her eyes as their lips met in the most perfect kiss. But then she pulled away. She had a weird feeling. Kind of like someone was watching them. She heard the sound of an ATV approaching and gasped. "It's Max and Big Joe! How did they find us?"

"Who cares? Let's fly!" Adam shouted, hopping down into the seat as fast as he could.

Shane turned the ignition and peeled out of there with the dust flying behind her.

"They're way behind us," Adam reported, turning around to look. "If we slam it, we'll be okay!"

Shane gripped the wheel tightly. She zoomed toward Lizzie and Marcus to warn them, but they were already on the fly themselves.

The ride was crazy, but they made it back to the bungalow before Max and Big Joe could get close enough to bust them. Shane hopped out of the ATV with Adam just as Lizzie and Marcus pulled up beside them.

"Close one," Lizzie said, panting. "How does Max keep finding us?"

Marcus shrugged, but Shane thought he had a weird look on his face. He probably felt guilty for setting up this date and taking the risk that they'd get into trouble.

Lizzie took a deep breath. "Guys. This is dangerous." She glanced over her shoulder to see if Max had caught up with them yet. "What we're doing . . . being together . . . we've got to stop."

"True," Shane agreed. "If we want to keep seeing each other, we have to keep it unromantic."

Adam's shoulders slumped, but he nodded.

"I know," Marcus said.

Lizzie nodded, too. "We have to. There are too many scholarships at stake."

"Okay," Marcus said, turning to leave. "Come on, Adam. We'll take the ATVs back."

"Wait!" Lizzie called, running after him. She stood on her tiptoes and leaned close to his face. "We can start unromantic in a minute," she said, then kissed him.

"How about in two minutes?" Adam called, walking back to Shane. He wrapped his arms around her waist and kissed her gently.

Yes! Shane thought, melting when she felt his soft lips. *How about if we start "unromantic" in three minutes?* she thought. *Or four? Or maybe next week!*

• • •

What am I doing? Marcus asked himself as he walked back to Max's production office that afternoon. His stomach was in knots because he knew what Max was going to say when he got there. He had messed up big-time.

I'm supposed to be setting up the sisters for all kinds of bad news on the show, Marcus realized. *Instead I'm dating one and covering for the other!*

I can't help it, he thought. *Lizzie's too special. And no job is worth my turning into a first-class slime-ball.*

He took a deep breath and walked into Max's office. Max was pacing the floor. Sasha sat in a corner with her feet up.

"What happened back there?" Max exploded, pointing out the window in the direction of the ATV course. "You were supposed to set it up so that we caught Adam and Shane in a romantic relationship! Can't you follow simple instructions?"

"I want this job," Marcus said firmly. "But you've gone too far, Max. Those girls don't deserve what you're doing to them."

"You mean what *we're* doing, don't you?" Max said. "*You* set them up for that date, Marcus."

It's true, Marcus thought. "You can do your own dirty work from now on," he said. "I'm out of it."

Max narrowed his eyes. "Fine. Then you're fired."

Is he kidding? Marcus thought. *He can't fire me for that!*

"Uh, Max," Sasha said from her chair in the corner. "We don't have any other interns. And I don't think we're going to find any by tomorrow. Not here in Mexico."

Max let out a loud sigh. "Okay. Then I'm demoting you to . . . sub-intern!"

Marcus turned to Sasha on his way out the door. "If I didn't need the money so badly for college, I'd have been out of here a week ago." He pushed open the office door and stormed out, almost knocking over Kelly in the hallway.

"What are you doing here?" Marcus asked her. Then he saw the stack of photos in her hands. He only got a glimpse, but they looked like pictures taken on the beach last night. Of Shane and Adam. "How and when did you get those?"

"None of your business," Kelly said, hiding the pictures quickly. "I'm here to see Max."

Uh-oh, Marcus thought. *I don't have a good feeling about this*. But there was nothing he could do. Nothing. Not if he wanted to keep his job.

CHAPTER NINE

"Hurry up," Lizzie called to her sister as the two of them got ready for the Campfire Council that night.

Shane had changed into a cute little Mexican cotton top that Lizzie had to admit looked awesome over her low-rise jeans.

Lizzie threw on a sundress, grabbed her cell phone, and went outside.

The two of them hurried to the pool, then down the torchlit path to the Campfire Council. Big Joe walked beside them the whole time, shooting close-ups of Shane.

Why is he in her face? Lizzie wondered as she headed toward the benches in the circle.

Kelly was already seated with the Aztec team's three totems stacked in her lap. JJ and Charles were on either side of her. Two more cameramen hovered with long lenses outside the circle.

Lizzie and Shane sat with Anthony and Justin.

"Welcome to the Campfire Council, Warriors," Max said. "First of all, congratulations to the Mayans for their clever win today in Survival of the Fittest. The score is now three to two, with the Aztecs leading by only one totem."

Kelly half sneered and half gloated from her bench. The campfire flames flickered, making her look like some kind of villain in a low-budget movie.

"Now about tomorrow's challenge," Max went on. "Without giving away too much, I'll tell you that it's all about balance."

"Excellent!" Lizzie cried. "Our little yogi, Shane, can out-balance anyone."

"However," Max interrupted them, "we have a situation on our hands. Two of our Warriors have been caught breaking the no-dating rule. And I have the pictures to prove it."

Lizzie glanced at Kelly, who was beaming smugly.

Max pulled a photo out of an envelope and held it up. It was a shot of Shane and Adam hugging on the beach. "According to our rules, Shane and Adam are disqualified from tomorrow's event," Max said.

A chorus of groans met the announcement.

When the Campfire Council was over, Lizzie and Shane strolled back toward the bungalow.

"I can't believe I got busted," Shane said. "It's usually *you* who gets into trouble."

"Me? What about the time you took your bike out at midnight because you wanted to chain yourself to that tree they were cutting down in the park?" Lizzie argued. "Mom and Dad were so worried about you."

"But the tree is still there," Shane said proudly.

"Yes, it is," Lizzie said. "I'll give you that." She

sat down by the edge of the pool, dangled her feet in the water. "How *is* Mom?" Lizzie asked quietly.

Shane joined her. "Mom? She's good. No, great. But she misses you a lot."

"Really?" Lizzie gulped.

"She wishes you'd come out to visit," Shane said softly.

From the tone in her voice, Lizzie thought maybe Shane was wishing the same thing.

"Dad always talks about you, Shane," Lizzie said. "He really misses *you*."

"I miss him," Shane admitted. "And to tell you the truth, sometimes I miss our old house. I mean, We *did* grow up there."

"Is that all you miss?" Lizzie held her breath, waiting, hoping Shane would say something nice.

At first Shane didn't answer. Then she glanced over at Lizzie. "I miss *this*," Shane admitted with a smile. "Being with you."

Lizzie reached out to give Shane a hug. "Me, too."

Shane hugged back. Then they both stood up.

"We'd better get some sleep," Lizzie said. "Tomorrow's a big day."

Shane laughed. "Are you ready for . . . *The Challenge?*" she asked, imitating Max as they walked into the bungalow.

"You bet I am!" Lizzie declared. *And I think I'm ready to be a sister again, too*, she thought.

• • •

"They've been balancing on totem poles in the ocean for two hours," Shane mumbled the next day. "How long does Max think they can stand there in the sun?"

Max sneered and turned to one of the cameramen. In the most dramatic voice he could muster, he said, "They've been standing out in the blazing sun for hours. How much longer can they survive without food or drink? That's entirely up to them because they *must* stick it out. That's why this show is called . . . *The Challenge!*"

"He's sick," Shane muttered to Adam, who was at her side.

So far Anthony, Justin, JJ, and Charles had all toppled off their totem poles. It had come down to a battle of wills between the toughest Warriors on each team—Kelly and Lizzie. But the two competitors were fading fast.

"Lizzie looks like she's going to faint," Adam said, nodding toward the water.

Wow, she does, Shane realized. Shane took a deep, calming breath and tried to send nothing but good vibes to her sister.

"Remember your breathing!" Shane called. "Focus! Find your inner *chi!*"

Lizzie smiled grimly from her stance. Shane could see that her sister's strength was beginning to give out. All at once Lizzie's knees buckled. She wavered, almost toppling into the water!

"Hang on!" Justin and Anthony gasped.

Kelly laughed while Lizzie flailed her arms, trying to keep her balance.

"Do your *ujjai* breathing, like I showed you!" Shane coached.

As if the words alone were enough to calm her, Lizzie seemed to suddenly relax her shoulders and regain her footing. She took a deep breath and managed to center herself on the pole. Then she closed her eyes and lifted her hands high above her head. Slowly, calmly, she brought her palms together and positioned her hands in front of her heart.

"Wow," Adam said. "She's really into it."

Lizzie lifted her left leg and extended it out in front of her, balancing on her right.

"I can't believe it," Shane said, full of pride. "She's doing it!"

Everyone onshore cheered.

"Hey, Kelly!" Shane called out. "Try that, why don't you?"

Adam laughed. "You think you can bait her that easily?"

Kelly immediately tried to lift one leg and balance the way Lizzie was doing. Almost at once she toppled sideways and fell into the water with a huge splash.

71

"Yup!" Shane said.

Lizzie shot a fist into the air triumphantly. "Mayans forever!" she shouted, then jumped into the water to cool off.

Shane, Justin, and Anthony darted down to the water and swam out to meet her. They splashed each other in a crazy, totally happy victory celebration.

"We won!" Lizzie cried. "We won!"

"Can you believe we're tied?" Shane said, feeling so happy she wanted to dance in the water.

"I know! All we have to do is keep it together for tomorrow," Lizzie said. "But right now I'm so hungry I could eat kelp."

"You don't have to eat kelp," Shane said. "Let's get out of here and go get our reward dinner!"

Lizzie showered and dried her hair faster than she'd ever done it before in her life. Then she hurried out to the deck by the pool. Shane, Anthony, and Justin were already sitting at a beautiful dining table. The Aztecs—Kelly, JJ, Charles, and Adam— were being forced to serve them the reward dinner as a punishment.

"You were awesome today!" Anthony said, taking several chicken quesadillas from a platter JJ was holding.

"Thanks!" Lizzie said. "Let's hope we win the final challenge tomorrow."

"Totally," Justin said. "Our entire college careers depend on our riding it fakie and pulling it on the backside air."

"Yeah," Lizzie said. "I guess so. Whatever that means."

For a few minutes no one talked. They were all too hungry and the food was delicious.

Shane looked over her shoulder and motioned to Adam. He was standing with the other Aztecs, who were dressed as Mexican waiters. "Oh, waiter," she called.

Adam grinned and hurried over. "You rang?"

"Yes," Shane said. "I could really use another Diet Coke."

Then she lowered her voice. "And I just wanted to tell you I miss you," she whispered.

"Ditto," Adam whispered back.

No fair, Lizzie thought. *Where's* my *forbidden love interest?*

Right on cue, Marcus pushed open the door from the bungalow and wandered outside.

"Hi," Lizzie said, finishing off her quesadilla and getting up to join him. The two of them wandered toward a private-looking area near some lighted cacti. Lizzie gazed up at the stars and sort of shivered with excitement. "Can you believe we won today? Only one more event and then . . . Georgetown, here I come!"

"Um, Lizzie," Marcus said, sounding serious. "That's what I wanted to talk to you about."

Lizzie searched his troubled eyes. "What? What is it?" she asked. She held her breath and waited for him to go on, but he didn't. Not until they were sitting on a bench, far enough away from the crowd so no one else could hear.

He cleared his throat but he wouldn't look her in the eyes. "I have something to say. I have to be honest with you."

"Tell me," she said, but by the sound of his voice, she wasn't so sure she wanted to know.

"It was my idea to put you and Shane on the show together," Marcus admitted.

"What?" she asked. It was the only thing she could think of to say out loud.

"I saw your audition tapes and took the concept to Max," Marcus explained. "Twin sisters who couldn't stand each other? It seemed like a really good . . . gimmick."

"A gimmick?" Lizzie repeated. Was that all she was to him?

"I thought it would be an innocent little ratings-grabber," he said. "I never dreamed I would *fall* for you."

Fall for me? How am I supposed to believe that? Lizzie wondered. *Maybe he was just saying* this *as a ratings grabber, too.* She shook her head, feeling awful. *How could I have been so wrong about him?* "I can't believe this," she muttered.

"Look, I know it's not an excuse," Marcus said, "but I need this job to pay for my college tuition. Believe me, I'll understand if you never want to speak to me again. I just had to tell you the truth."

"I'm such an idiot," Lizzie said.

"No, you're not," Marcus said. "You're smart and fun and beautiful, and I'm crazy about you."

"So why are you telling me this now?" Lizzie asked.

"Because I couldn't stand being dishonest with you," Marcus said. "Because Max will do anything for ratings. And because in tomorrow's challenge . . . I know he's going to try to mess with you and Shane again. Lizzie, I—" Marcus reached for her.

But Lizzie stood up quickly. "I'd thank you, but I think it's a little late for honesty, Marcus," she said. "And I really don't know how I feel about you right now."

She walked away, past the pool, past her sister and the others having dinner, heading straight down to the beach. She didn't want anyone to see her cry.

Shane hurried to catch up with her. "What's wrong?" she asked, concerned. "Did something happen with Marcus?"

Lizzie nodded, her throat tight. For a minute she

didn't want to talk, and Shane knew it. She knew enough to just wait.

Finally Lizzie told her the whole thing.

"I just can't believe it," Lizzie said when she was through. "He's such a liar."

Shane wrapped an arm around her. "I'm really sorry he turned out to be such a weasel," she said.

Lizzie shrugged, trying to convince herself she didn't care. But she could feel tears building up in her eyes. "Whatever," she said. "This was supposed to be about college scholarships, not falling in love."

"Right," Shane agreed. "And no matter what happens tomorrow . . . or even after tomorrow . . . no matter what Max throws our way . . . we have each other."

Lizzie smiled even as a tear spilled onto her cheek. "We do, don't we?" she said.

CHAPTER TEN

"Warriors, today is the final and most important day of competition," Max announced. "It's been a grueling week. A week of tough challenges and heart-stopping triumphs. You've put your bodies and minds on the line. But it all comes down to this moment. This event. This challenge we call . . . the Warrior Relay!"

Shane rolled her eyes. *Get over yourself, Max*, she thought. *Let's get this thing going!* She checked out the other players. Kelly's face was tight and fierce. Charles seemed worried. Even Adam looked like he was stressed about the outcome.

But JJ looked as if she couldn't wait for this all to be over so she could sign up for the show she had *intended* to go on—*American Starmaker*.

Beside her, Shane felt Lizzie nervously reach out and give her hand a squeeze.

"This event requires you to demonstrate the skills of a great warrior: speed, bravery, cunning, and intellect," Max went on. "If during any portion of this event you fall, you must go back and begin that portion again." Max smiled and looked each Warrior in the eye. "There's a lot riding on this. So go forth, Warriors—and may the best team win!"

A conch shell sounded, and both teams took off running, following the signs for the relay event. The first sign led them to the pool, where two floating pontoon bridges had been stretched from one end to the other.

"Come on, Mayans!" Anthony shouted, cheering Shane as she stepped onto a bridge.

Anthony, Justin, and Lizzie wobbled a little, but they made it across it without falling.

On the far side of the bridge Shane found a piece of parchment with a map leading to their next move. "Down those stairs to the beach!" she shouted, running as fast as she could. Behind her she heard a loud splash as one of the Aztecs fell into the pool.

"What is wrong with you people?" she heard Kelly shout.

The map led them to a Jet Ski launch. Sasha was waiting with instructions. "Ride out to those flags on the buoy!" she told them. "Each of you grab a puzzle piece attached to a flag!"

Justin hopped on the Jet Ski first and hotdogged it into the waves. He circled the buoy, grabbing the first flag and puzzle piece without stopping.

Lizzie went for the next flag, followed by Anthony, then Shane.

"We're doing this!" Shane cheered, giving her puzzle piece to Justin.

Justin put it together with the other three. "This

way!" Justin said, running down the beach in the opposite direction. Soon they came upon two rope suspension bridges stretched across a deep canyon.

"Oh, no," Shane said, feeling her heart pound in her chest. Her head started spinning.

"What?" Anthony called, racing to the bridges.

"She's afraid of heights!" Lizzie cried, glancing at Shane as she ran.

Shane stood at the edge of the cliff, looking down. Fierce waves crashed on the jagged rocks below. A sign at the entrance to the bridge read: ONE AT A TIME. BRIDGE WILL NOT SUPPORT TWO PEOPLE.

"Come on!" Justin said. "We've got to get across! The Aztecs are catching up!"

Shane looked over her shoulder. The Aztecs were in the distance, racing toward them.

She stepped up to the edge of the bridge. Justin and Anthony had already raced across. Lizzie was crossing it now, and almost at the far side.

Just do it, Shane thought, trying to make herself follow Lizzie. But the fear was too much.

"I can't," Shane said, gripping the rope on both sides. "I'm sorry. I just can't."

Lizzie watched her sister stare in sheer terror at the canyon below. She had to help Shane . . . somehow. "You can do this," she coached her. "Come on. Just don't look down!"

Shane took two terrified steps onto the rope bridge and froze again. Her hands gripped the rope railings.

A hundred yards away Kelly's team had reached the second bridge, and they were crossing it.

"I can't!" Shane cried, her voice cracking.

"You have to!" Lizzie pleaded. "Come on—our future's in your hands! Do your Fuji breathing!"

"It's *ujjai* breathing!" Shane said.

"Whatever it's called—just do it!" Lizzie begged.

Shane closed her eyes, and for a moment Lizzie couldn't tell what was happening. Either Shane was trying to calm herself . . . or she was stuck in a complete panic attack.

"Shane?" Lizzie said in a whisper so soft no one could hear it. "I know you can do this."

Shane's eyes opened a moment later, and she took a single step forward. Then another. Slowly, she made it across the bridge.

Lizzie cheered, giving her sister a high five before the two of them raced off to follow Justin and Anthony.

The team scrambled to the last leg of the relay.

Lizzie's heart leaped. Ahead of them was the final totem—the prize. It sat in the middle of a barren mound of land surrounded by a shallow pit. All she had to do was walk across a wooden plank and they'd win!

But when she reached the pit, her heart almost stopped. The pit was filled with slinky, slimy black snakes, all twisted around each other, all slithering toward her with their tongues lashing out!

Justin and Anthony had already walked the plank and were waiting for her on the other side.

Shane hurried across, too. Then she whirled around. "Oh, no! You're afraid of snakes!"

"I can't do it." Lizzie choked out the words.

"Lizzie, the totem is *right here*. This is just Max messing with our heads! We can't let him win!" Shane argued.

I know, Lizzie thought. *Max and Marcus. But it's snakes!* She shivered just thinking about them. "I can't do it!"

"Yes, you can!" Shane encouraged her. "They're just water snakes. They're not poisonous! I read it in the *Worst Possible Situations Handbook*."

Lizzie's eyes opened wide. "You *read* the book?"

"*Of course* I read it!" Shane said. "I read it last night because I knew it was important to you."

Wow. Lizzie couldn't believe how good that made her feel. *Okay*, she thought. *Maybe I can do this.*

"Take baby steps," Shane called. "Do it slowly!"

Slowly? Lizzie thought. *No way!*

She took a deep breath and ran across the wooden plank. "Ahhhhh!"

"We did it!" Shane cheered, hugging her sister.

"We won!" Lizzie cried, dancing around, then hugging Justin and Anthony, too.

The guys grabbed the totem off of a small pedestal and hoisted it high into the air.

"M.I.T., here I come!" Justin cried.

"Our champion Warriors!" Max walked toward them with Big Joe in tow. "Congratulations, Mayans. This has truly been the most exciting *Challenge* ever!"

Lizzie went for another round of hugs with her teammates. It was so great to celebrate together. And amazing to know that she'd be getting her scholarship to Georgetown!

Finally, though, it was time to head back to the resort—and then home. The camera crew stopped taping and packed up their gear.

"Lizzie?" a voice from behind her called, just as she was making her way to an ATV. She whirled around and saw Marcus.

I was hoping he'd turn up, she thought. Except she still didn't know how she felt about him. Or what she'd say.

"I just wanted to say congratulations," he said. "You deserve this." He handed her a piece of paper.

"Thanks," she said. "What's this?"

"Something I wanted you to see," he answered. "It's a copy of the letter I gave Max this morning. I quit the show."

"But how will you pay for college?" she asked.

"Not *this* way," Marcus said firmly. "I'll figure out something."

A huge, happy smile spread across Lizzie's face. "Marcus, I think I've decided how I feel about you," she said, leaning close enough to kiss him.

He wrapped his arms around her, and she felt his lips meet hers. *Now* this *is what I call winning big-time!* she thought.

"Hey," Marcus said. "Check it out." He nodded toward Shane and Adam, who had their arms around each other, too.

"Let's break up that party," Lizzie joked, pulling Marcus with her.

"Sorry you didn't get the scholarship," Shane was saying to Adam.

"Oh, don't worry about me," Adam said. "I'm probably going to get a baseball scholarship anyway."

"You are?" Shane's eyes popped open wide. "To Stanford?"

"Yup," Adam said. "So if you're at Berkeley, we'll be just an hour apart."

Shane beamed at him, and they kissed again.

"Hey, break it up, you two," Lizzie joked. "Marcus and I have one more challenge for you."

"We do?" Marcus shot her a questioning look. "That's the first I've heard about it."

"I just thought of it," Lizzie said with a twinkle in her eye. "Come back to the resort, and I'll tell you all about it."

CHAPTER ELEVEN

"He's coming!" Lizzie called to Marcus and Adam. "Are you guys ready?"

Lizzie, Shane, Marcus, and Adam were at the spot on the beach where they'd answered questions for Don't Spill the Beans. The huge bucket still hung overhead on its wooden support structure.

"You bet!" Adam called, holding a rope to the bean pot. Marcus stood in front of Adam, hiding him.

"Good." Lizzie glanced at Shane. "You know the drill, right?"

Shane nodded. A grin spread across her face as she held up a disposable camera. "Ooh, here comes Max now!" she said.

She and Shane walked up to Max and flashed him a totally innocent, starstruck smile. "Can we talk?" Lizzie asked him.

"Sure," Max said. "What is it?"

"You're such a big star," Shane said. "My sister and I were wondering, could we get your picture in front of one of *The Challenge* events? For our friends back home?"

"Okay." Max grinned, acting all full of himself for doing this little favor for his fans. "Listen, I hope there are no hard feelings about the show. It was just good TV."

"Oh, we understand completely," Lizzie said.

Shane waved a hand, motioning for Max to move a little to the left. Then a little more. A little more.

Perfect! Lizzie thought. *He's right under the pot!*

Shane held the camera up to her eye. "Say beans!" she said.

"Beeeeeans," Max said, grinning from ear to ear.

Shane snapped the shutter, and at the same time Adam pulled the rope. With a huge whoosh, the bucket tipped over, splattering gallons of beans on Max's head!

"Arrgh!" he cried, his white linen clothes suddenly covered in wet black slime.

Lizzie, Shane, Adam, and Marcus laughed so hard, they almost knocked each other down.

Then Big Joe stepped out from a hiding place in the bushes.

"Got it, Big Joe?" Shane called to him.

"Got it," Big Joe said, giving them a thumbs-up sign.

"Now *that's* what I call good TV!" Lizzie declared, and the four of them walked off, arm in arm, down the beach.

BOOK SERIES

Based on the hit television series

Mary-Kate and Ashley are off to White Oak Academy, an all-girl boarding school in New Hampshire! With new roommates, fun classes, and a boys' school just down the road, there's excitement around every corner!

Coming soon wherever books are sold!

Don't miss the other books in the TWO of a kind book series!

- ❏ It's A Twin Thing
- ❏ How to Flunk Your First Date
- ❏ The Sleepover Secret
- ❏ One Twin Too Many
- ❏ To Snoop or Not to Snoop?
- ❏ My Sister the Supermodel
- ❏ Two's A Crowd
- ❏ Let's Party!
- ❏ Calling All Boys
- ❏ Winner Take All
- ❏ P.S. Wish You Were Here
- ❏ The Cool Club

- ❏ War of the Wardrobes
- ❏ Bye-Bye Boyfriend
- ❏ It's Snow Problem
- ❏ Likes Me, Likes Me Not
- ❏ Shore Thing
- ❏ Two for the Road
- ❏ Surprise, Surprise!
- ❏ Sealed With A Kiss
- ❏ Now You See Him, Now You Don't
- ❏ April Fools' Rules!
- ❏ Island Girls
- ❏ Surf, Sand, and Secrets

- ❏ Closer Than Ever
- ❏ The Perfect Gift
- ❏ The Facts About Flirting
- ❏ The Dream Date Debate
- ❏ Love-Set-Match
- ❏ Making A Splash!
- ❏ Dare to Scare